IN NOVEMBER

Harcourt, Inc.

San Diego   New York   London

Printed in Singapore

IN NOVEMBER

Cynthia Rylant

ILLUSTRATED BY *Jill Kastner*

For my mother
—C. R.

For Leah and Mack
—J. K.

In November, the earth is growing quiet. It is making its bed, a winter bed for flowers and small creatures. The bed is white and silent, and much life can hide beneath its blankets.

In November, the trees are standing all sticks and bones.
Without their leaves, how lovely they are, spreading
their arms like dancers. They know it is time to be still.

In November, some birds move away and some birds stay. The air is full of good-byes and well-wishes. The birds who are leaving look very serious. No silly spring chirping now. They have long journeys and must watch where they are going.

The staying birds are serious, too, for cold times lie ahead. Hard times. All berries will be treasures.

In November, animals sleep more. The air is chilly and they shiver.

Cats pile up in the corners
of barns.

Mice pile up under logs.
Bees pile up in deep, earthy holes.

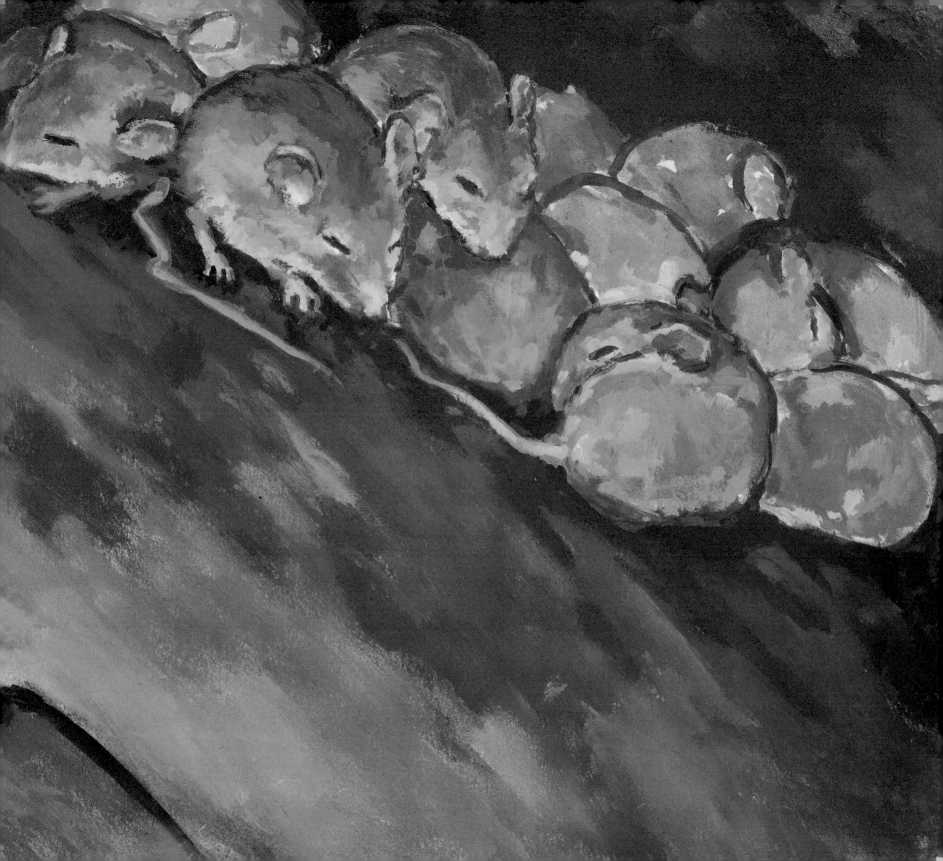

And dogs lie before the fire.

In November, the smell of food
is different. It is an orange smell.
A squash and a pumpkin smell.
It tastes like cinnamon and can
fill up a house in the morning,
can pull everyone from bed in
a fog. Food is better in November
than any other time of the year.

In November, people are good
to each other. They carry pies
to each other's homes and
talk by crackling woodstoves,
sipping mellow cider.

They travel very far on a special November day just to share a meal with one another and to give thanks for their many blessings—for the food on their tables and the babies in their arms.

And then they travel
back home.

In November, at winter's gate, the stars are brittle. The sun is a sometime friend. And the world has tucked her children in, with a kiss on their heads, till spring.

www.harcourt.com

Library of Congress Cataloging-in-Publication Data
Rylant, Cynthia.
In November/Cynthia Rylant; illustrated by Jill Kastner.
p. cm.
Summary: Describes the autumn activities and traditions that
November's cooling temperatures bring.
[1. Autumn—Fiction.] I. Kastner, Jill, ill. II. Title.
PZ7.R982In 2000
[E]—dc21   98-22276
ISBN 0-15-201076-9

G H

The illustrations in this book were done in oil on paper.
The display type was set in Poetica.
The text type was set in Berling.
Printed and bound by Tien Wah Press, Singapore
Production supervision by Pascha Gerlinger
Designed by Lydia D'moch